MW01273407

COUNTRIES IN THE NEWS
PAKISTAN

Kieran Walsh

Rourke
Publishing LLC
Vero Beach, Florida 32964

www.rourkepublishing.com

The country's flag is correct at the time of going to press.

PHOTO CREDITS:
All images © Peter Langer Associated Media Group

Title page: Pakistanis crowd onto a train in the Punjab province.

Editor: Frank Sloan

Cover and interior design by Nicola Stratford

Library of Congress Cataloging-in-Publication Data

Walsh, Kieran.
  Pakistan / Kieran Walsh.
      p. cm. — (Countries in the news.)
Includes bibliographical references and index.
Contents: Welcome to Pakistan — The people — Life in Pakistan—
School and sports — Food and holidays — The future — Fast facts —
The Muslim world.
  ISBN 1-58952-680-5 (hardcover)
 1. Pakistan—Juvenile literature. [1. Pakistan.] I. Title. II. Series.

  DS376.9.W35 2003
  954.91—dc21

                                                    2003005668

Printed in the USA
CG/CG

TABLE OF CONTENTS

Welcome to Pakistan...4

The People...8

Life in Pakistan..12

School and Sports 14

Food and Holidays...16

The Future 19

Fast Facts..20

The Muslim World 21

Glossary 22

Further Reading...23

Websites to Visit..23

Index..24

WELCOME TO
PAKISTAN

Pakistan is a large country in Asia. It is also one of the world's most crowded countries. Almost 150 million people live there. At its widest point, Pakistan is about 2,800 miles (4,500 kilometers) across.

Snow-capped mountains tower over a stream in Pakistan's beautiful landscape.

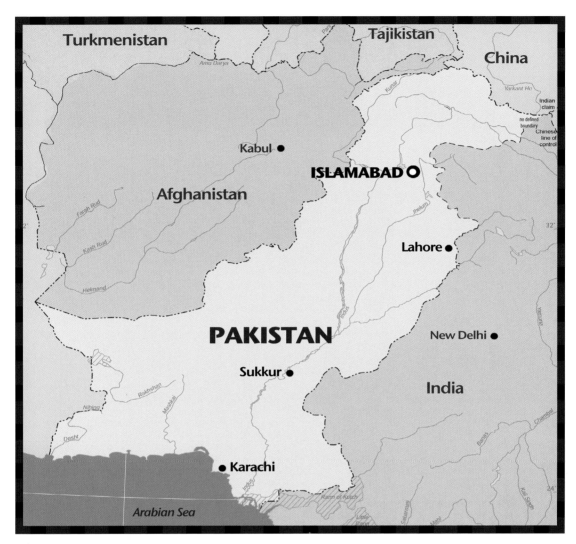

Afghanistan lies to the west, and India is to the east. Pakistan is about the size of the states of Oklahoma and Texas combined.

The land is varied. In the north there are many very tall mountains. The most famous is known as K-2. It is 28,250 feet (8,611 meters) high. K-2 is the second highest mountain in the world, after Mount Everest.

Pakistan also has large amounts of desert. And there are miles of beaches along the Arabian Sea. The mountains of the west are separated from farmland in the east by the **Indus** River. The Indus was home to a famous ancient civilization. People have lived in this part of the world for many centuries.

Pakistan became a country in 1947. Until then, the land had been part of the country of India. Pakistan was formed to make a homeland for **Muslims**, followers of the **Islam** religion.

Karachi is Pakistan's largest city. It is a seaport and the country's financial center. The capital of the country is Islamabad. It is a new city, built in the 1960s.

A street scene in Karachi

THE PEOPLE

People who live in Pakistan are known as **Pakistanis**. Almost all Pakistanis are Muslims. Because the country is so large, Pakistanis speak different languages, depending on where they live. The country's official language is **Urdu**, although more and more people are learning to speak English.

Children cluster into a three-wheeled taxi in Lahore.

A Pakistani drives a donkey cart filled with hay.

Many of Pakistan's people live in small villages. These people work long hours as farmers or laborers in factories. The people who live in cities often may have a large number of people living in a small apartment. No matter where they live, the family is very important to Pakistanis.

Military life is important to Pakistanis. In some parts of the country, many of the men have jobs as soldiers.

Men and women spend little time together. They are generally not seen together on the streets or in public places.

An Army officer in Lahore

LIFE IN PAKISTAN

Both men and women often wear pants that taper at the ankles and loose shirts outside the pants. These shirts hang just below the knees. Many women cover their faces when they appear in public.

In large cities, there are always crowds and plenty of traffic jams. Almost always, however, you see only men on the streets. Women mostly stay at home and visit among their neighbors.

Men wear traditional clothing.

A typical street scene in a Pakistani village

SCHOOL AND SPORTS

Most children who live in the countryside do not go to school. They are needed at home to help with the farming. Many of those who do go to school don't go beyond the fifth grade. This is because there are very few schools. Many people in Pakistan cannot read or write. There are also very few colleges or universities in Pakistan.

! Some of the most popular sports in Pakistan are soccer, field hockey, and cricket. Cricket is popular because India and Pakistan were once part of the British Empire.

Many children in Pakistan would rather play in a pool than go to school.

FOOD AND HOLIDAYS

Food is important to most Pakistanis, and they prepare elaborate meals. Many kinds of spices are used to make the food tasty. Lamb and chicken are popular meats. They are often grilled and served on **kebabs**. **Dhal** is a sauce made of lentils and is served almost everywhere. Several kinds of bread are served, and Pakistanis eat many meals by wrapping their food in these breads.

Ramadan is a month-long Muslim holiday, during which people have to **fast** during the day. The holiday that ends Ramadan is called **Id ul Fitr**. It is a happy time when families get together to exchange presents and eat large meals.

A food vendor sells food on the street in Lahore.

Young and old gather together in a small village in Pakistan.

THE FUTURE

Although many Pakistanis are poor, they have a fairly high standard of living. Pakistan, however, is growing too quickly and cannot always feed its people.

Pakistan also needs to improve its education. More children need to attend school, and the country needs to open more high schools and colleges.

More and more Pakistanis are moving to the cities. As cities become more crowded, the country needs to provide better housing.

They face many challenges, but Pakistanis are extremely hard-working and **devout** people. They may yet be able to take control of their lives.

FAST FACTS

Area: 300,700 square miles
(778,753 square kilometers)

Borders: Iran, Afghanistan, China

Population: 147,663,429
Monetary Unit: rupee

Largest Cities: Karachi (10,132,000);
Lahore (5,452,000); Islamabad (636,000)
Government: Republic

Religion: Sunni Muslim 77%; Shiite Muslim 20%
Crops: rice, wheat, cotton

Natural Resources: natural gas
Major Industries: textiles,
food processing, beverages

THE MUSLIM WORLD

There are more than 1,200,000,000 Muslims in the world. Only Christians, with 2,000,000,000 people, are a bigger religion.

Almost two thirds of Muslims live in Asia and Africa. There are two major groups of Muslims: 16% of them are Shiite and 83% are known as Sunni.

Muslims follow the Islam religion. Muslims believe in God, who they know as Allah. The religion was begun around AD 610 when Muhammad became known as a prophet. He wrote down his teachings in a holy book called the Koran.

GLOSSARY

cricket (KRICK et) — an English game, still often played in Pakistan

devout (dee VOUGHT) — very serious, reverent

dhal (DOLL) — a sauce made of lentils

fast (FAST) — to go without food, usually for religious reasons

Id ul Fitr (ID UHL FIT ur) — a holiday celebrated at the end of Ramadan

Indus (IND us) — the main river of Pakistan

Islam (IZ lahm) — the religion followed by Muslims

Karachi (kuh ROTCH ee) — Pakistan's largest city

kebabs (KUH bawbz) — meat grilled on a skewer

Muslims (MUZ lumz) — people who follow the religion of Islam

Pakistanis (PACK uh STAN eez) — natives of Pakistan

Ramadan (RAM uh DAN) — the ninth month of the Muslim year

Urdu (UHR DOO) — the official language of Pakistan

FURTHER READING

Find out more about Pakistan with these helpful books:

- Clayton, Elspeth. *Pakistan.* Rigby Interactive, 1997.
- Deady, Kathleen W. *Pakistan.* Bridgestone Books, 2001.
- Marchant, Kerena. *Muslim Festival Tales.* Raintree Steck Vaughn, 2001.

WEBSITES TO VISIT

- paknews.com/
- www.un.int/pakistan/

INDEX

Arabian Sea   6

Asia   4

dhal   16

education   14

Id ul Fitr   16

Indus River   6

Islamabad   6

K-2   5

Karachi   6

kebabs   16

Muslims   6, 8

Ramadan   16

Urdu   8

About the Author

Kieran Walsh is a writer of children's nonfiction books, primarily on historical and social studies topics. A graduate of Manhattan College, in Riverdale, NY, his degree is in Communications. Walsh has been involved in the children's book field as editor, proofreader, and illustrator as well as author.